YAY FOR VAYCAY!

Flora Ahn

SCHOLASTIC PRESS / NEW YORK

Library of Congress Cataloging-in-Publication Data available

ISBN 978-1-338-11847-6

10 9 8 7 6 5 4 3 2 1 19 20 21 22 23

Printed in the U.S.A. 23

First edition, February 2019

Book design by Yaffa Jaskoll and Mary Claire Cruz

To my mom and dad, the best
pugsitting grandparents ever

CHAPTER 1

Sunny and Rosy started off the morning with their usual routine.

After breakfast—and after-breakfast snack—Sunny and Rosy said goodbye to their human. They prepared for a busy day of napping, neighborhood surveillance, yoga stretches, and watching their favorite show, *Officer Bert: Paws on Crime*.

They were in the middle of their yoga stretches when their human came home early and surprised them.

They ran to greet her, but slid to a stop when they saw that she wasn't alone.

A strange creature floated behind their human and into the house.

"Intruder! Intruder!" the pugs cried.

Sunny hid behind the curtains, but Rosy barked to scare the creature away.

"Silly pups," said their human. "It's just a suitcase." She opened it up.

"Is a suitcase a kind of bed?" Rosy whispered to Sunny. She hopped inside. "I hope not. It's not comfy at all."

Sunny nudged Rosy aside to try it out. "You're right."

Their human tipped Sunny and Rosy out of the suitcase and rolled it into her bedroom. She began filling it with her clothes.

"Look," Sunny said. "Our human is making it squishier for us."

Sunny and Rosy hopped into the suitcase again, pawing at their human's clothes to get their new bed just right.

"Sunny! Rosy! That's not for you!" Their human shooed them out of the suitcase.

"Maybe this is a bed for someone else?" Rosy whispered to Sunny. "Maybe we're getting another sister? Or maybe a brother!"

Sunny wished hard for Rosy to be wrong. She loved Rosy, but one sibling was enough for her.

CHAPTER 2

To Sunny's relief, no new sister or brother puppy appeared when she opened her eyes.

But their human began packing up *their* bed and favorite toys.

When their human carried the large bin filled with their food outside, Sunny and Rosy started to panic.

FOOD

Their human came back in and picked up their harnesses and leashes. The jingle of their leashes made Sunny and Rosy forget for a second about their worries.

But, instead of heading down to their usual walking path, their human plopped them into the back seat of the car.

"Where do you think we're going?" Rosy asked. "I hope it's not the vet."

Sunny poked her nose outside the window and took three big sniffs. "I'll know where we're going soon."

After a long drive, Sunny's tail started to slowly wag. "Ooh, this smells kind of familiar. I think I know where we are!"

Before Sunny could say more, the car slowed in front of a large house.

While
their
human
carefully
lifted Sunny
out of the car
and placed her
gently on the grass,
Rosy hopped out and ran in circles,
frantically investigating this new location.

The door to the house flew open and an elderly couple waved at them.

"Welcome to Grandma and Grandpa's house!" their human cried.

"Oh, Princess Sunny!" Grandma said. Sunny beamed as she received face massages and butt scratches.

Grandpa turned to Rosy. "This must be Princess Rosy. Well, that means Sunny gets promoted to Queen!"

Sunny smirked at Rosy as they were ushered into the house in a flurry of hands, paws, and tangled leashes.

Their human gave the elderly couple a hug. "Hi, Mom! Hi, Dad! Thank you for watching Sunny and Rosy. I'll be back in two weeks."

"Two weeks," Rosy yelped. "That's forever!"

Sunny nudged Rosy. "Don't complain so much. Just follow whatever your queen does and you'll be fine." Sunny tried to sound confident, but she had never stayed here longer than a few days before and was a little worried.

Their human gave Sunny and Rosy a big hug. "I'll miss you so much. You two are the best dogs in the whole world. Listen to Grandma and Grandpa—and be good!"

Before Sunny and Rosy could lick her cheek, their human was gone.

Rosy moped by the door. Sunny went to join Grandma and Grandpa to set a good example for Rosy, but she couldn't stop her tail from drooping out of its curl.

CHAPTER 3

Sunny and Rosy spent the afternoon curled up next to Grandpa as they all watched a movie called *The Hound of the Baskervilles*. Grandpa liked watching Detective Sherlock Holmes and Dr. Watson solve the mystery, but Sunny and Rosy liked barking at the scary hound.

After the movie finished, Grandma patted Sunny and Rosy on their heads. She opened the door to the backyard. "Want to help with the gardening?" she asked.

Sunny sped to the door. Rosy trailed after Sunny. "What's so great about a garden?" she mumbled.

But Rosy had never been
in a garden like this before.

"No eating or digging," Grandma said before kneeling on a small cushion by one of the vegetable beds. "You can explore the garden, and if you're good, I'll make you a big barbecue feast at the end of the week!"

SUNNY AND ROSY'S FAVORITE THINGS ABOUT THE GARDEN **TOP 5**

5. All the delicious fruits and vegetables that Grandma would cook for them!

4. Shrubs shaped like animals.

3. So! Many! Flowers!
2. The birds and bees.
1. The fountain.

After a full afternoon of playing in the garden, Sunny and Rosy stretched out on the soft grass and watched Grandma weed until they fell asleep.

But their nap was soon interrupted.

"Oh no!" Grandma cried.

Sunny and Rosy sat up and looked around.

Dark green and purple leaves from the rows of cabbage, spinach, kale, and lettuce were half-eaten. Several dozen tomatoes had bite marks. Any squash, pear, nectarine, or fig within a few feet was either partially eaten or completely gone.

"This is very bad," Grandma said, shaking her head. "I thought I could trust you in the garden, but now it's ruined. There will absolutely be no barbecue feast now."

She shooed them inside
and closed the door behind them.

Sunny whirled around to face Rosy. "How could you ruin the garden like that!"

Rosy raised her paws in the air. "It wasn't me. Paws crossed!"

"Okay, I believe you," Sunny said. "But if it wasn't either of us, who was it?"

Neither of them knew the answer to that question, so they sat by the glass door and watched Grandma clean up.

"We have a mystery on our paws. You know what we have to ask ourselves, right?" Sunny said.

"What would Officer Bert do?" Rosy danced in excitement.

"No," Sunny said. "What would Detective Sherlock Holmes and Dr. Watson do!"

Sunny and Rosy stayed up late that night watching more Sherlock Holmes and Dr. Watson movies.

"Let's watch one more," Sunny said, her mouth full of cookies. "For research."

Rosy nodded and scooted closer to Sunny to grab a big pawful of popcorn from the bowl.

CHAPTER 4

The next morning, after Grandma and Grandpa left the house, Sunny and Rosy got right to work solving the mystery. Their first stop was a box of old Halloween costumes Sunny had spied in the basement on her last visit.

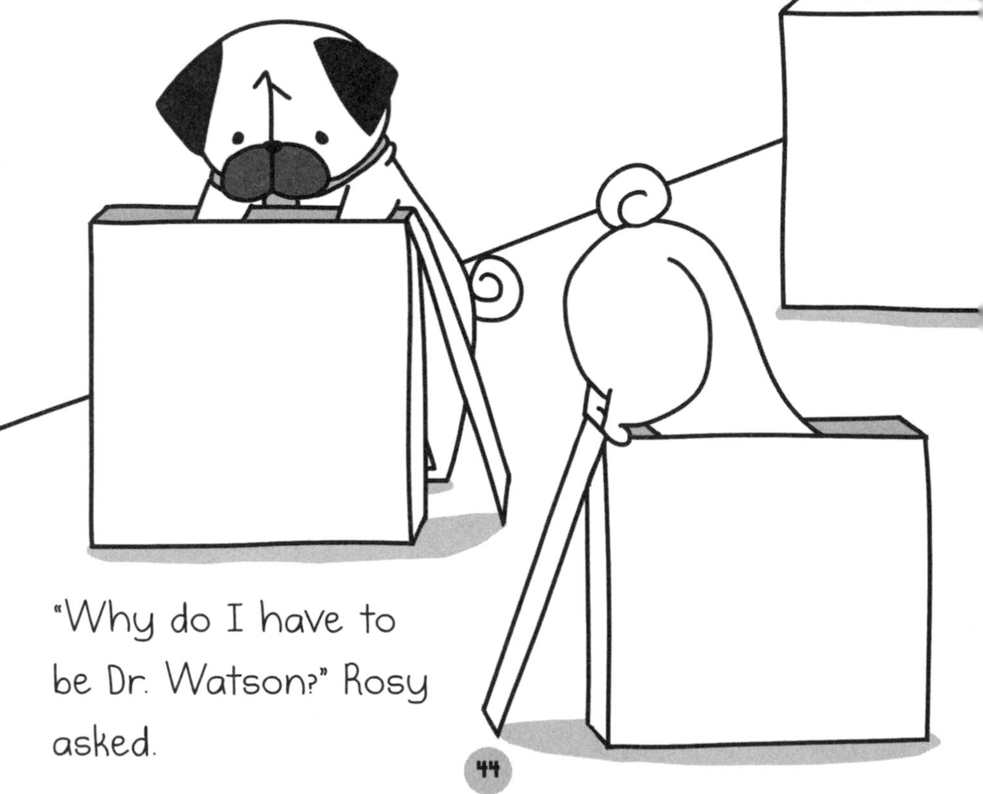

"Why do I have to be Dr. Watson?" Rosy asked.

"I'm older so I get to decide," Sunny said. "And besides, I knew you'd want the mustache."

Rosy twirled the mustache.

Together, they opened the back door that Grandma had left unlocked. Sunny took out a large magnifying glass and peered at the damaged fruits and vegetables in the garden.

After they had finished investigating the yard, Sunny gestured to Rosy. "You go first. What do you see?"

Rosy pointed at the bare stalks in the vegetable patch. "The bite marks here look like they were made by two very big front teeth."

"And look at these. Paw prints!" Sunny said. "These were definitely made by the thief."

"How do you know that?" Rosy asked.

"Elementary, my dear Rosy," Sunny said. "Count the number of toes in the back paw prints."

"Five!" Rosy shouted.

"Yes, and we only have four toes," Sunny said. "So that means someone else was here recently.

"We need to set a trap and catch the thief in action," Sunny continued. "All we need is the right bait."

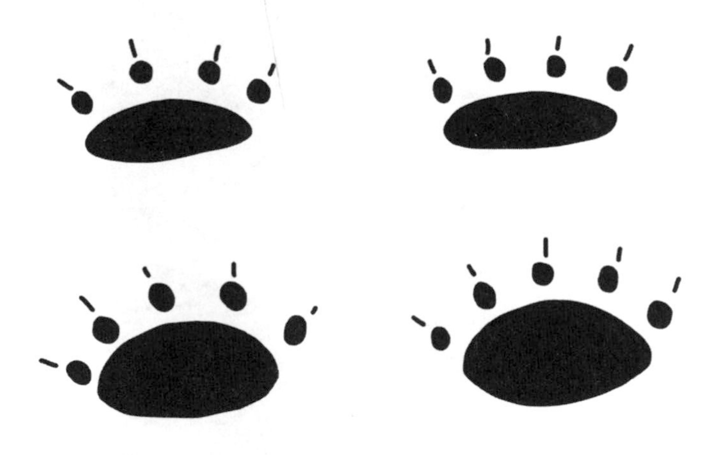

Sunny pointed at the crushed and half-eaten pieces of fruit hidden in the grass. "Look at what the thief ate."

"The thief ate everything," Rosy said.

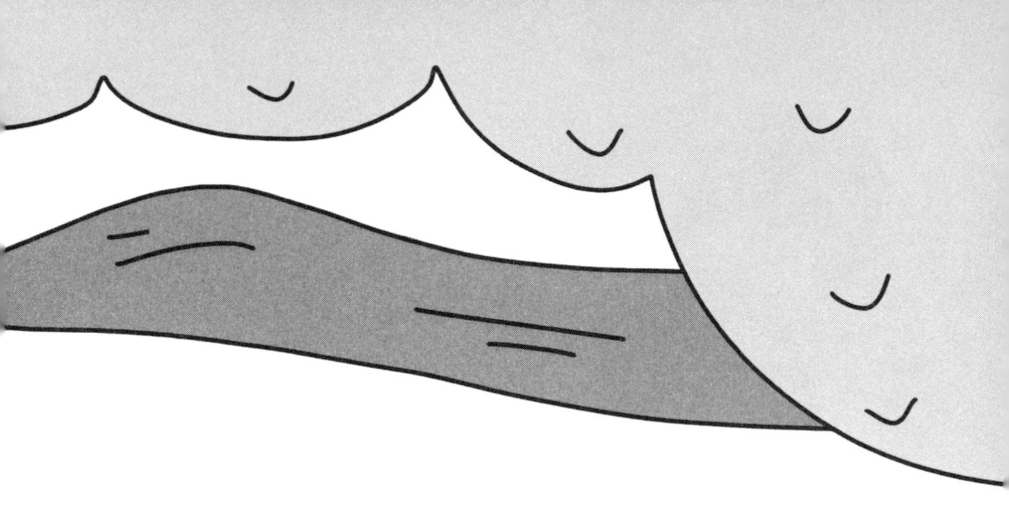

"Yes," Sunny said. "The thief tasted a little bit of everything. But the thief ate all of this." She held up a peach pit. "This is what the thief loves best. So we just need to get some more peaches for our trap."

Sunny and Rosy had to use teamwork to reach the peaches in the tree.

Then they laid a trap with the juicy peach and hid behind a blueberry bush.

"How long is this going to take?"

"What if the thief never shows up?"

"Do you think we can eat some of these blueberries while we wait?"

Rosy didn't stop with the questions until Sunny shushed her.

"I don't know, we'll try again tomorrow, and no you can't eat these blueberries," Sunny said.

SHHH!

CHAPTER 5

An hour later, they were almost about to give up, when they heard a rustling sound.

They peered around the bush.

"Excuse me, what are you two looking at?"

Sunny and Rosy jumped and spun around.

A little brown groundhog was munching on blueberries, his whiskers twitching with each bite.

"Who are you?" Sunny asked.

"Clover. Nice outfits!" Clover said. "Are you going to a costume party?"

"We're doing a stakeout," Rosy said. "We're going to catch a thief."

Clover gasped. "What did the thief take?"

"Someone stole a bunch of fruits and vegetables from Grandma's garden," Rosy said.

"That's just terrible," Clover said. "I hope that you catch whoever it is. Good luck!"

Sunny and Rosy waved goodbye to Clover as he waddled off.

Grandma and Grandpa were due home any minute, so Sunny and Rosy went back inside and changed out of their clothes.

"I guess the thief is gone." Rosy jumped onto Grandpa's armchair to relax.

"I don't think so." Sunny stared out the glass door. "Look!"

The peach in their trap had been eaten and all that was left was a bare pit.

CHAPTER 6

The next day, Sunny and Rosy were disappointed to wake up to rain.

They tried setting a new trap, but the storm was too ferocious.

The rain continued for two more days. Sunny and Rosy tried to find ways to amuse themselves while they waited.

3, 2, 1.
Ready or not,
here I come!
No!
And the
ghost had
eaten all
the food!

Miss.
A4?

You sunk
my battleship!

Finally, the rain stopped. After Grandma and Grandpa left the house, Sunny and Rosy returned to the garden and set another trap.

Then they waited.

And waited.

And waited.

They were both struggling not to fall asleep when they heard a noise that made them jump.

Clover made his way toward them. "Did you catch the thief yet?"

"No," Rosy said.

"That's a shame," Clover said. "Did you set another trap? I want to hear all about your plan. Wait right there while I grab a snack first."

Clover waddled away and returned with a pile of food in his arms. He bit off two large pieces of a peach and held them out to Rosy. "These peaches are the best in the county," Clover said. "I can smell them a mile away!"

"Thank you," Rosy said as she took a big bite. "This is delicious!"

Sunny frowned. She peeked behind the blueberry bush.

Sunny swatted the peach out of Rosy's paws.

"Hey!" Rosy yelled.

"Don't eat that," said Sunny. "Don't you see? Those are the peaches from the trap! Clover's the thief!"

"Thief?" Rosy shouted. "Thief!"

Sunny and Rosy lunged at Clover.
"I thought we were friends! This isn't friendly behavior!"

He flew into the air and then popped into the ground.

"Where did he go?" Rosy asked.

"There!" Sunny said.

They chased after Clover.

But soon, he disappeared into a nearby hole for good.

"We'll try again tomorrow," Sunny said, panting.

CHAPTER 7

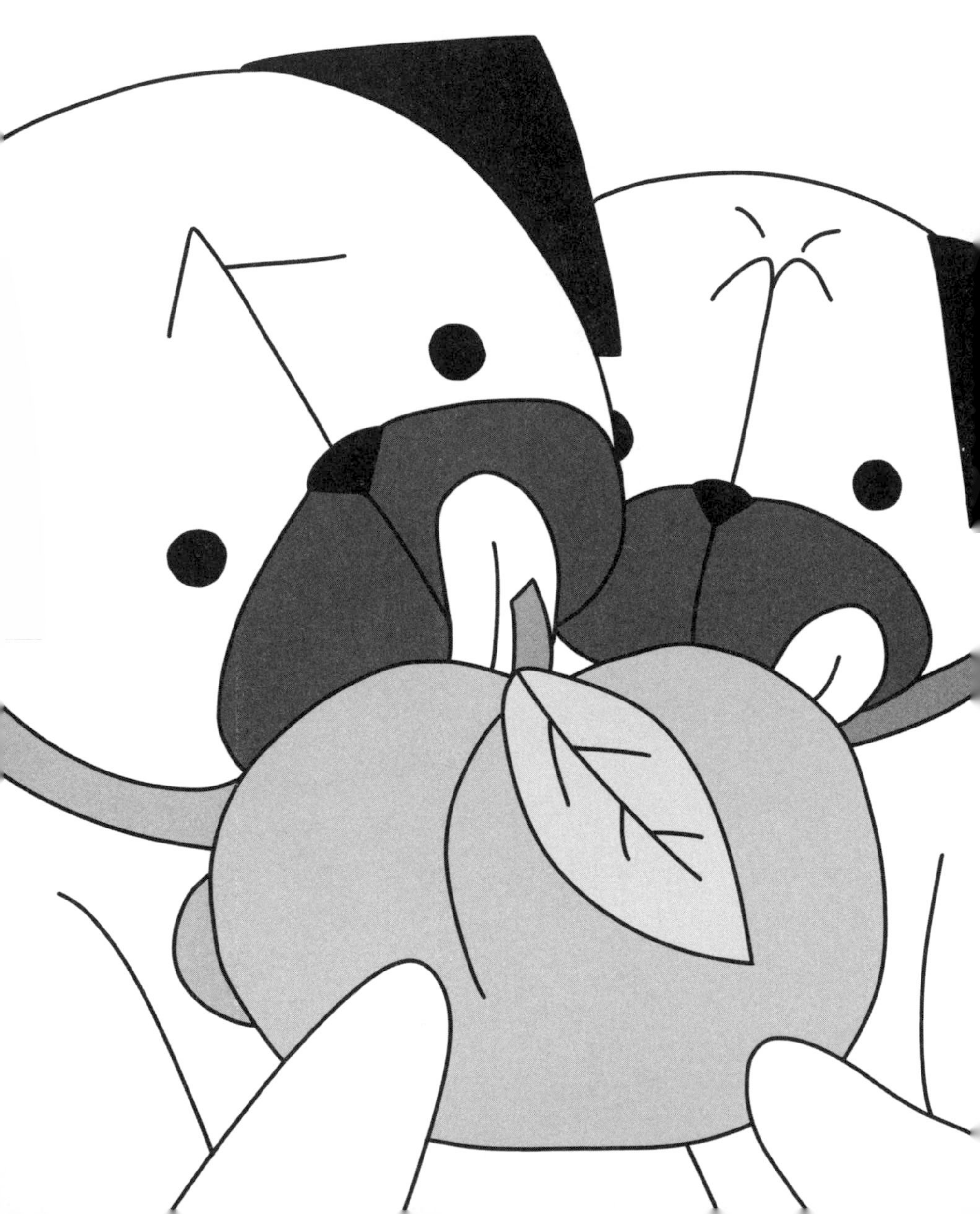

The next day, Sunny and Rosy set the juiciest peach they could find just next to the groundhog hole and waited.

It only took a few minutes before they heard scratching and sniffing sounds.

As Clover emerged from the hole, Sunny and Rosy leaped on top of him.

"Got you, thief!" Sunny shouted.

"This is downright rude. I'm not a thief," Clover said, trying to squirm out of their hold. "Let's talk like civilized groundhogs."

Sunny and Rosy released him, and Clover sat up and brushed himself off. "Now, what's all this nonsense?"

"You ate half of Grandma's vegetables and fruits," Sunny said.

"I did," Clover said. "And they were delicious."

"That's stealing!" Rosy shouted.

Clover shook his head. "She plants food, and I eat food. That's what food is for."

Rosy scratched her ear. "When you put it that way, it sounds okay."

Sunny sighed. "No! Clover, you ate Grandma's food without asking for permission first. That's stealing. Not only that, but she thinks we did it! You got us into trouble."

Clover's nose twitched. He burst into loud sobs. "I hadn't thought of it that way. Oh dear."

Clover covered his face with his paws. "I am the thief! I'm so sorry. How will you ever forgive me?"

Rosy burst into tears too and hugged Clover. "You're a good groundhog," she cried. "You didn't know. It's okay. We forgive you!"

Sunny waited for Rosy and Clover to finish crying. "Clover, we still want to be your friends and we're not mad at you. But you can't keep stealing our grandparents' food."

"I understand," Clover said. "I'll stick to the nearby woods like before. And I'll help you prove your innocence. I have an idea . . ."

CHAPTER 8

The next day, Sunny and Rosy waited eagerly for Grandma to put on her gardening hat and gloves.

"No, no," Grandma said to them as she opened the door. "You can't go outside with me. Don't want another mess now, do we?"

Sunny and Rosy sat down and watched through the glass door as Grandma walked through her garden.

"Do you see him?" Rosy asked.

"Shh," Sunny said. "Not yet."

When Grandma turned to weed her cucumbers, Clover finally popped out from his hole.

Then he waddled over to the archway.
This was Sunny and Rosy's signal.

They barked their loudest barks and pawed at the door.

Grandma looked up and shushed them. But Sunny and Rosy didn't stop until Grandma turned to see what they were barking at.

There was Clover, climbing the archway.

Grandma shrieked and ran toward him. Clover dangled in midair for a moment and then leaped into a pot of Grandma's prized begonias.

Clover winked at Sunny and Rosy.

He sped down the vegetable rows.

He snapped up bites of everything he passed.

Just before Grandma could catch him, he made his getaway by diving back into his hole.

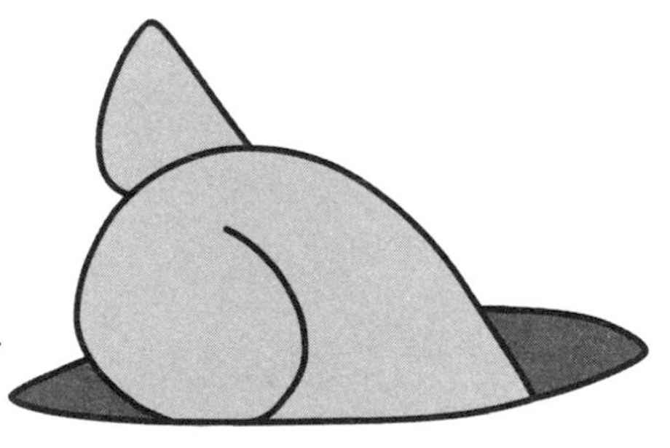

"Such good little pups!" Grandma patted Sunny and Rosy on their heads. "Thank you for alerting me to that groundhog. I'm sorry I thought you were the ones

eating my garden. Looks like you've earned your barbecue feast after all!"

That night, Grandpa and Grandma grilled beef, hot dogs, zucchinis, squashes, and green beans outside.

Sunny and Rosy ate so much, their bellies grew round.

"Best watchdogs ever," Grandpa praised them.

For the rest of the week, Sunny and Rosy enjoyed their outside time with Grandma as she tended to her garden.

On the pugs' last day, Sunny and Rosy had a *Paws on Crime* marathon. It was interrupted by a surprise guest . . .

"Sunny! Rosy! I missed you so much!" Their human rushed in to greet them.

Sunny and Rosy jumped up and licked their human's face.

The pugs had been having such a good time, they had forgotten when she was coming back!

Grandma and Grandpa hugged Sunny and Rosy goodbye. Their human struggled to put on their harnesses. They were a little snug after a week of delicious snacks.

The pugs
waddled to the
front yard and their
human grunted as she lifted
them into their seats.

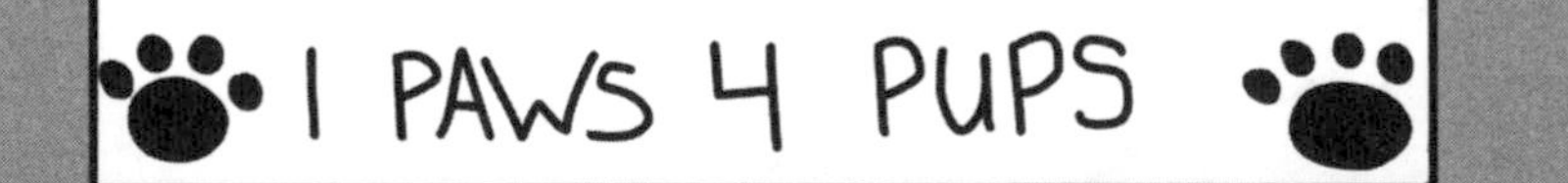

As their human started their car, Sunny and Rosy waved out the window to Grandma and Grandpa.
PUG MOBILE

TOP 5
SUNNY AND ROSY'S TOP 5 FAVORITE THINGS ABOUT GRANDMA AND GRANDPA'S HOUSE
5. Making new friends.
4. Relaxing outside.

3. Snuggly movie time with Grandpa.
2. Playing in the grass.
1. BBQ feasts!

As soon as Sunny and Rosy returned home, they started their own garden.

Rosy was impatient for their plants to grow.

She kept a daily watch until they were ready for picking and eating.

"I know just who would love this!" Rosy cried.

To: Clover
We miss you!
Enjoy this gift from
our garden!
Sunny & Rosy

Flora Ahn is an attorney by day, but by night, she's the author and illustrator of the cartoons on her blog, *Bah Humpug*. Although she tried to draw other things, her pugs, Sunny and Rosy, insistently barked and pawed at her until she made drawings of them. Lots and lots of drawings of them. She lives in Virginia, where she spies on her pugs and uses her observations to develop her blog and books.